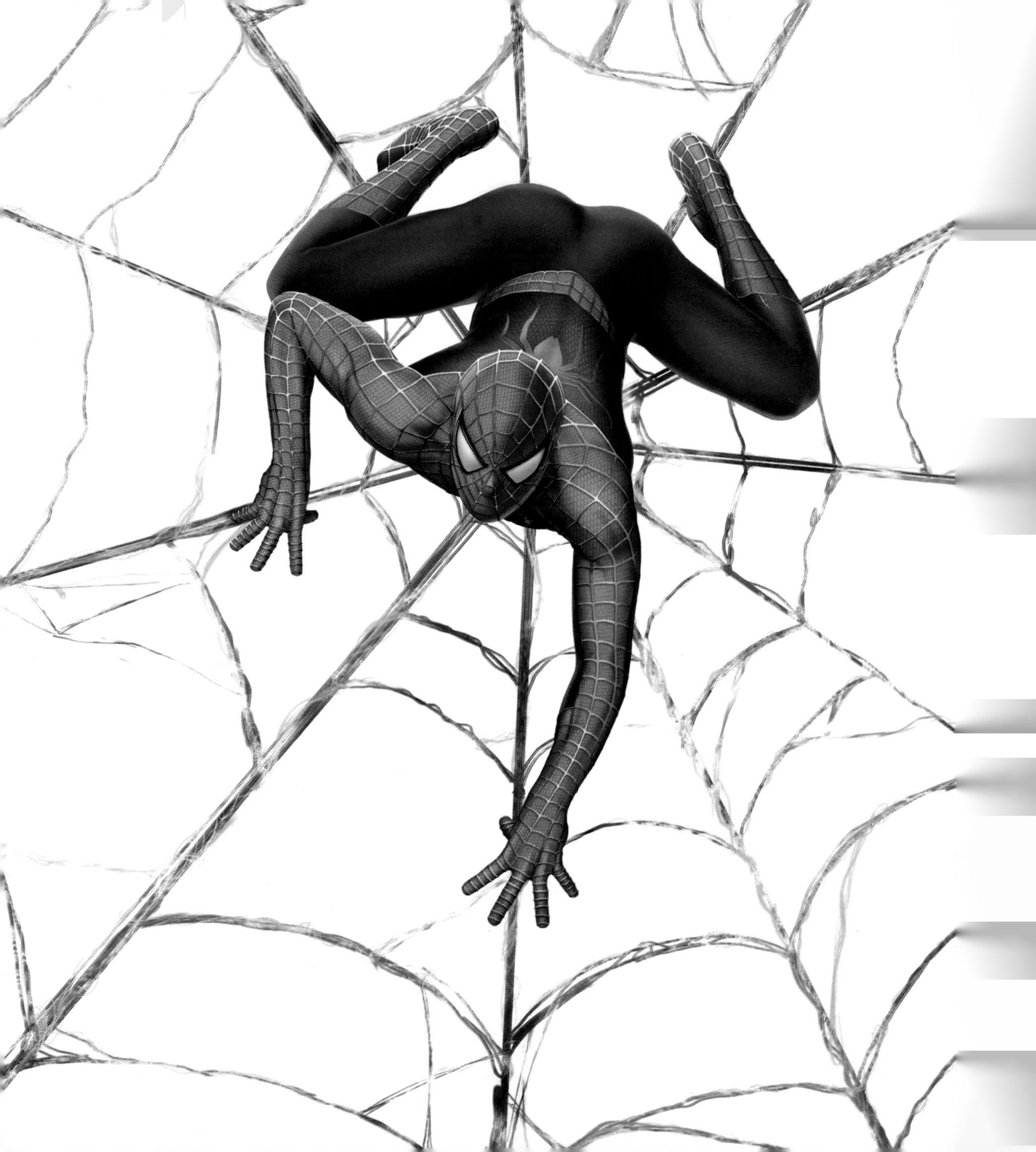

COLUMBIA PICTURES PRESENTS A MARVEL ENTERPRISES / LAURA ZISKIN PRODUCTION
TOBEY MAGUIRE "SPIDER-MAN"2" KIRSTEN DUNST JAMES FRANCO ALFRED MOLINA ROSEMARY HARRIS DONNA MURPHY
MUSIC BY DANNY ELFMAN EXECUTIVE PRODUCERS STAN LEE & KEVIN FEIGE EXECUTIVE PRODUCER JOSEPH M. CARACCIOLO BASED ON THE MARVEL COMIC BOOK BY STAN LEE AND STEVE DITKO
SCREEN STORY BY DAVID KOEPP AND ALFRED GOUGH & MILES MILLAR SCREENPLAY BY ALVIN SARGENT PRODUCED BY LAURA ZISKIN AVI ARAD DIRECTED BY SAM RAIMI
MARVEL   SPIDER-MAN CHARACTER TM & © 2004 MARVEL CHARACTERS, INC. ALL RIGHTS RESERVED.   sony.com/Spider-Man   COLUMBIA PICTURES

Spider-Man 2: Hands Off, Doc Ock!

HarperCollins®, 🖊️®, and HarperFestival® are registered trademarks of HarperCollins Publishers Inc.
No part of this book may be used or reproduced in any manner whatsoever without written permission except in the case of brief quotations embodied in critical articles and reviews. Printed in the United States of America. For information address HarperCollins Children's Books, a division of HarperCollins Publishers, 1350 Avenue of the Americas, New York, NY 10019.
Library of Congress catalog card number: 2003113595
3   4   5   6   7   8   9   10
❖
First Edition
www.harperchildrens.com
www.sony.com/Spider-Man

Hands Off, Doc Ock!

Adapted by Kate Egan

Illustrations by Isidre Mones, Jose Antonio, and Bob Ostrom

Based on the Motion Picture

Screenplay by Alvin Sargent

Screen Story by Alfred Gough & Miles Millar and Michael Chabon

Based on the Marvel Comic Book by Stan Lee and Steve Ditko

HarperFestival®
A Division of HarperCollins*Publishers*

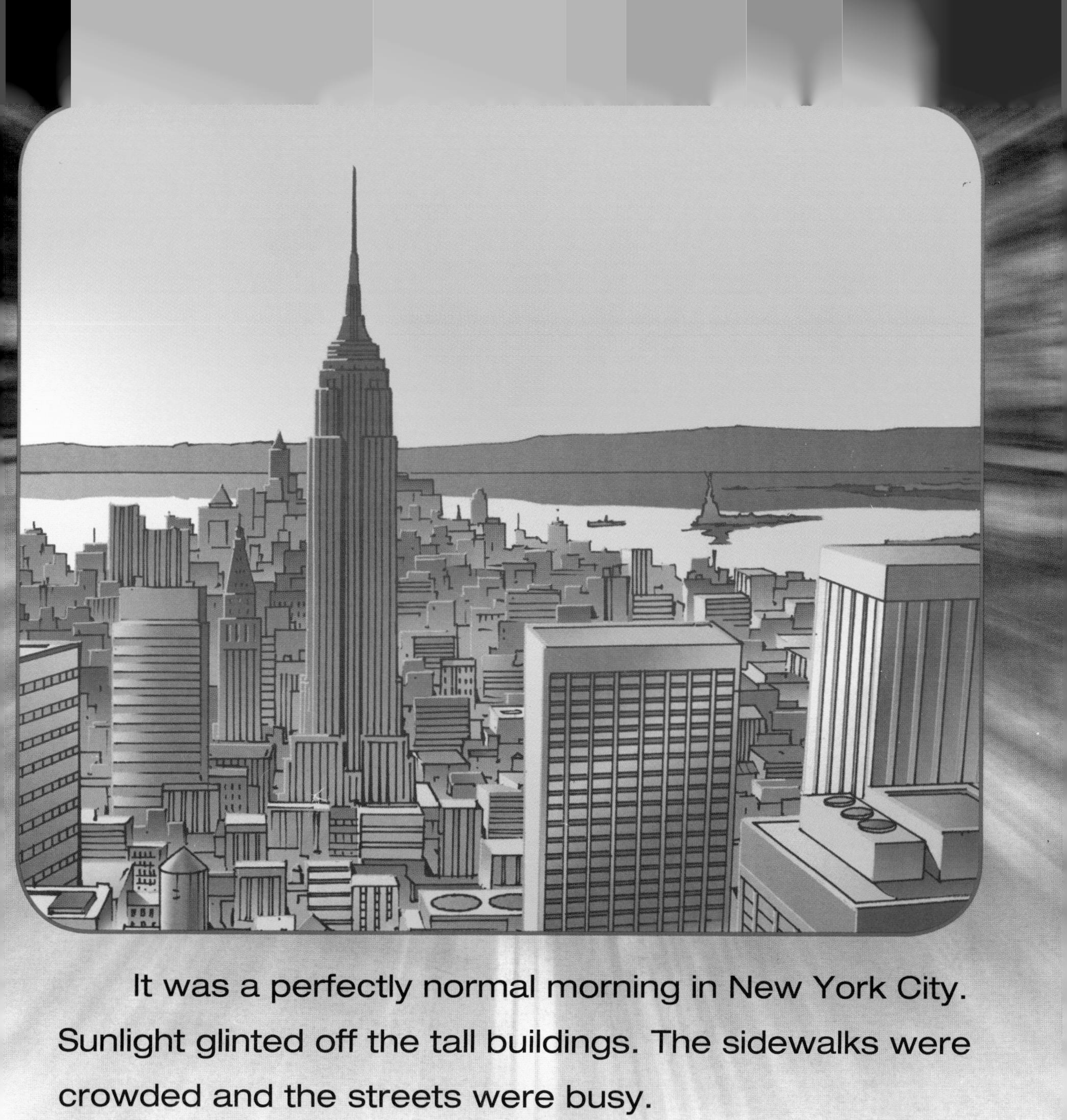

It was a perfectly normal morning in New York City. Sunlight glinted off the tall buildings. The sidewalks were crowded and the streets were busy.

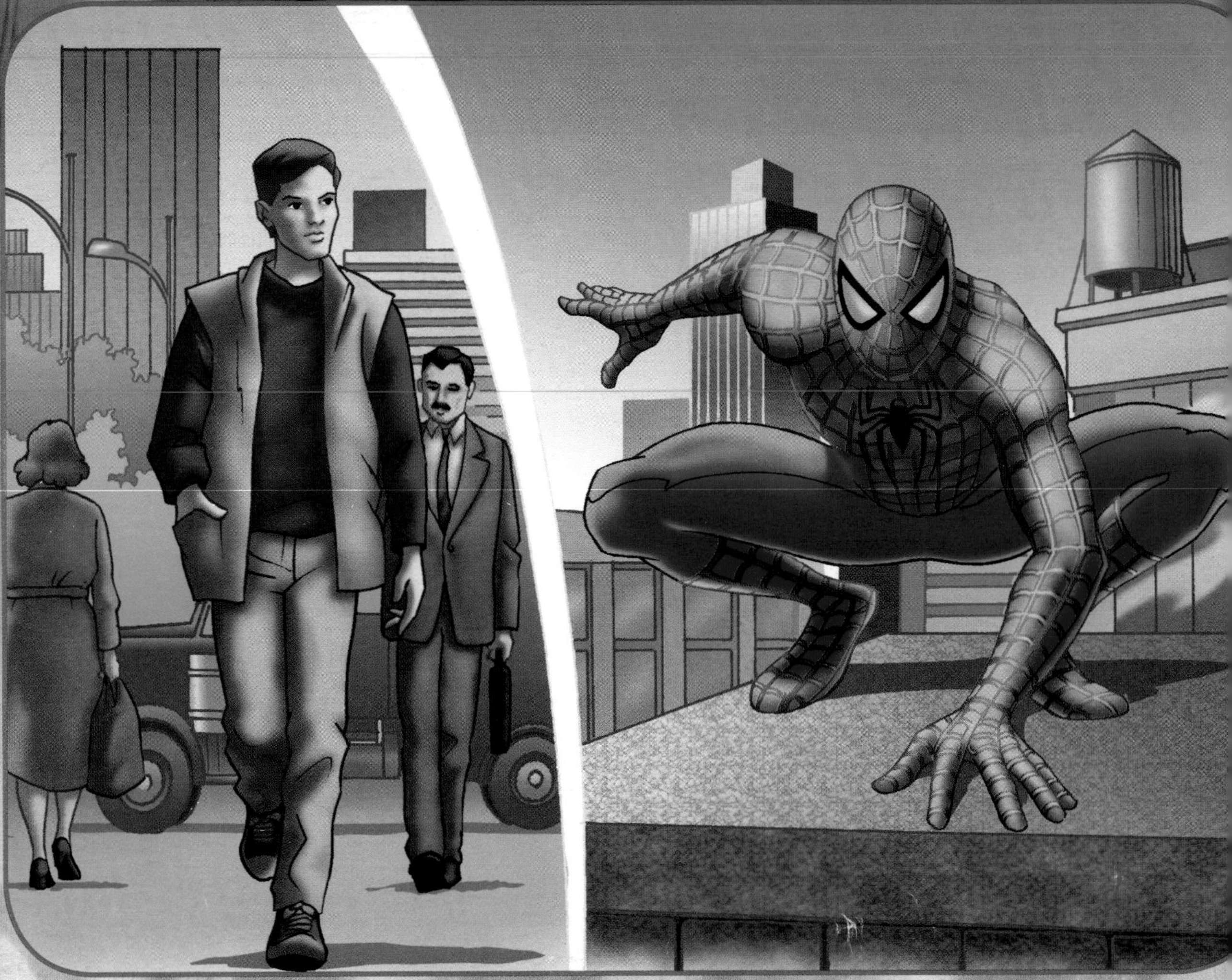

It was a perfectly normal morning for Peter Parker, too. But normal for him was a little different. Peter lived a double life: Sometimes he was a regular guy and sometimes he was Spider-Man! Peter never knew when he'd have to swoop in to stop a crime.

One day Peter was in line at the bank, waiting to take out some money. Suddenly his spider sense kicked in! He knew danger was near and warned the other customers. Most of them huddled together on the floor.

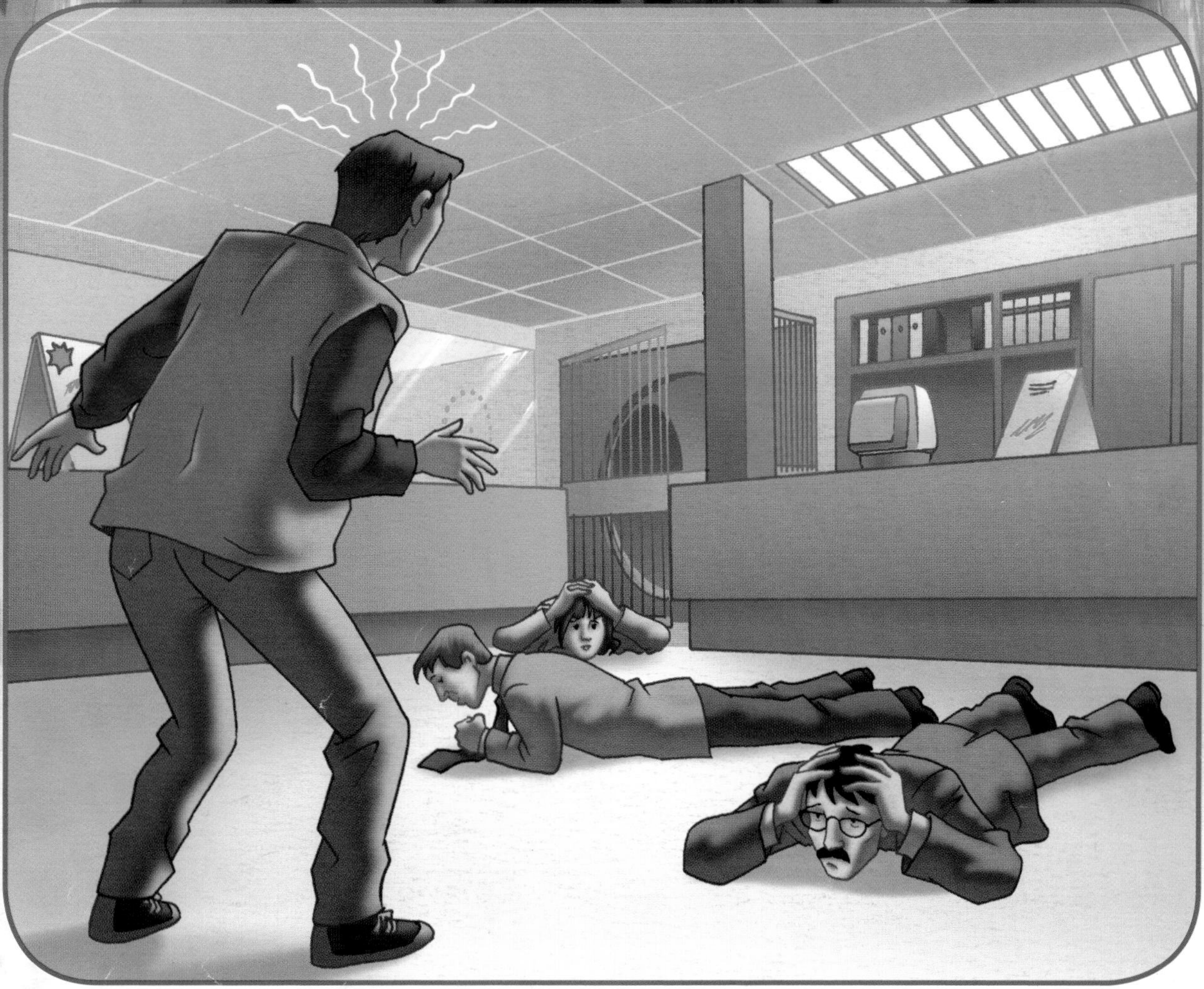

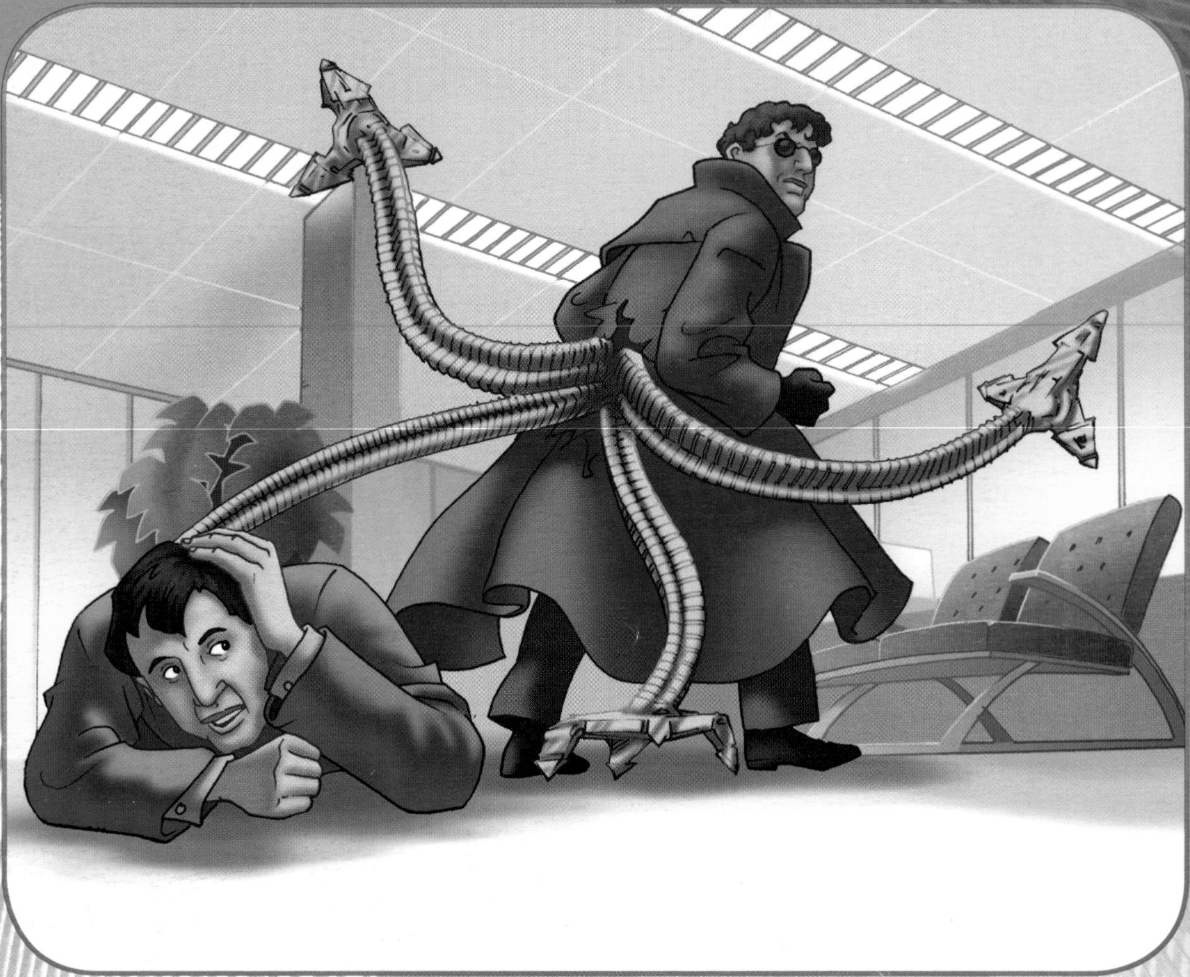

But one of them was standing up!

Peter wanted to warn him that he was in danger, too. Before he could say anything, four metal tentacles ripped out of the man's coat!

He wasn't a customer at all! He was the new villain in town, Doc Ock. He was robbing the bank! Peter knew it was time for Spider-Man to help out.

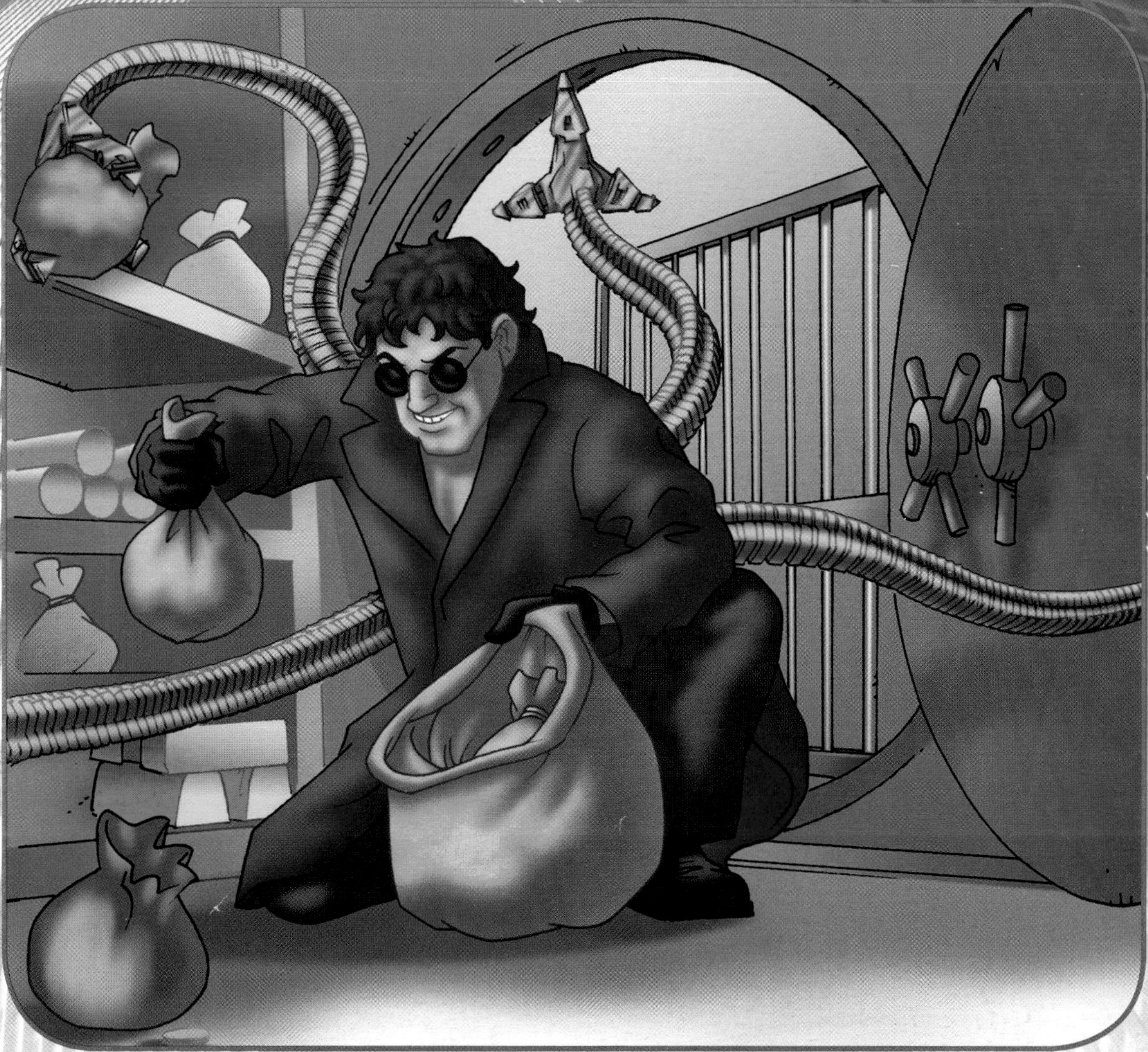

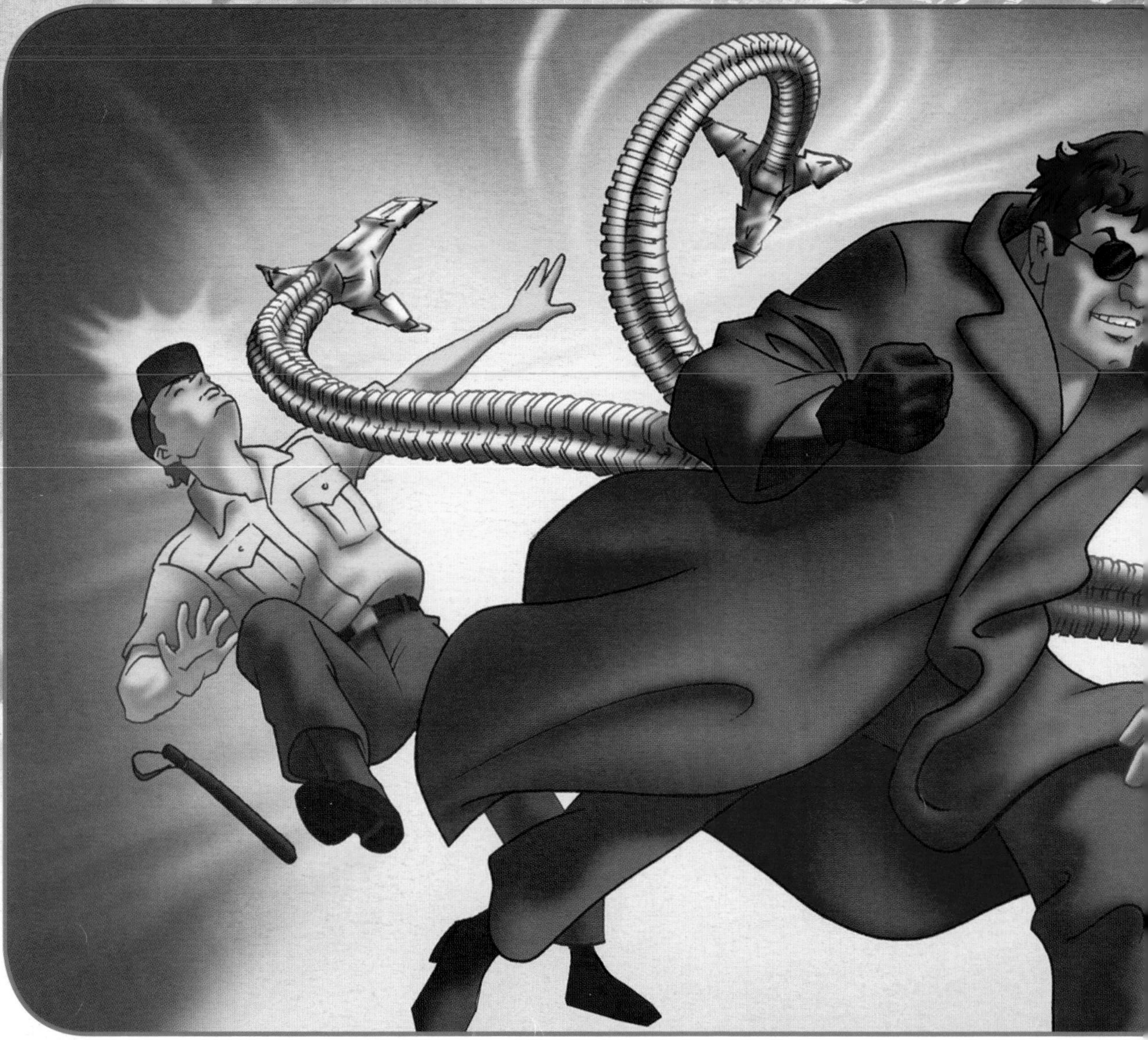

Doc Ock was once a famous scientist. But one of his experiments had gone terribly wrong. Now he had four deadly tentacles fused to his body!

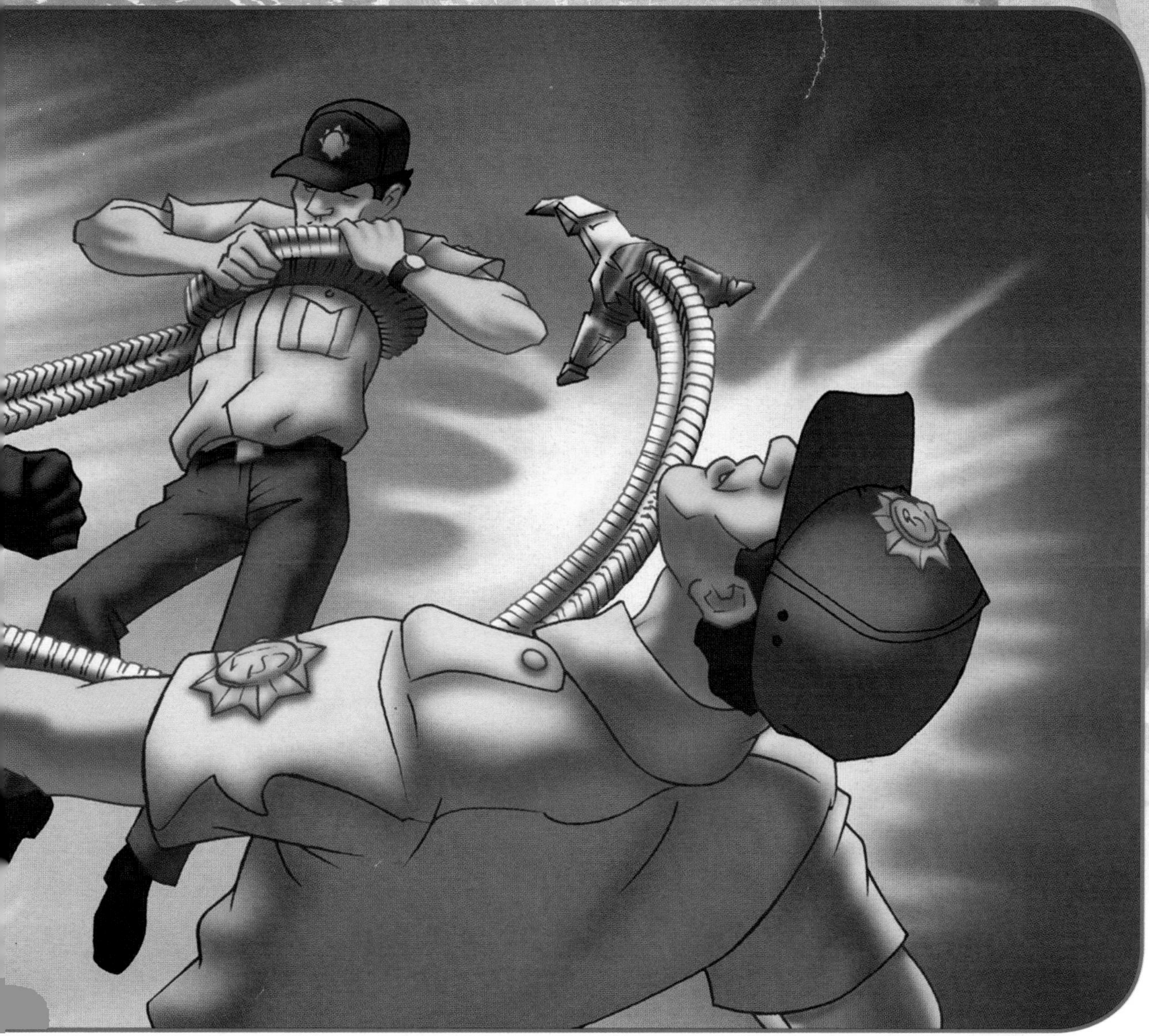

Doc Ock used his extra limbs to slash and crush his victims.

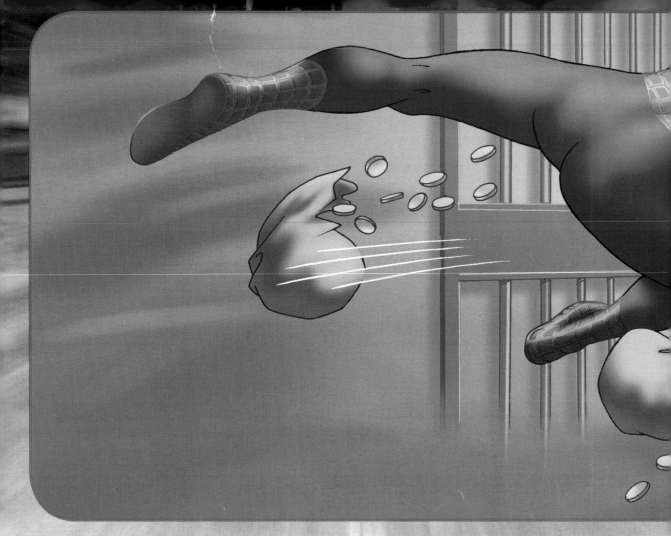

Spider-Man to the rescue! Peter put on his suit and leaped into action.

"How dare you interfere with me, Spider-Man," Doc Ock growled. He hurled heavy bags of coins at Spider-Man. Spider-Man dodged one and then another.

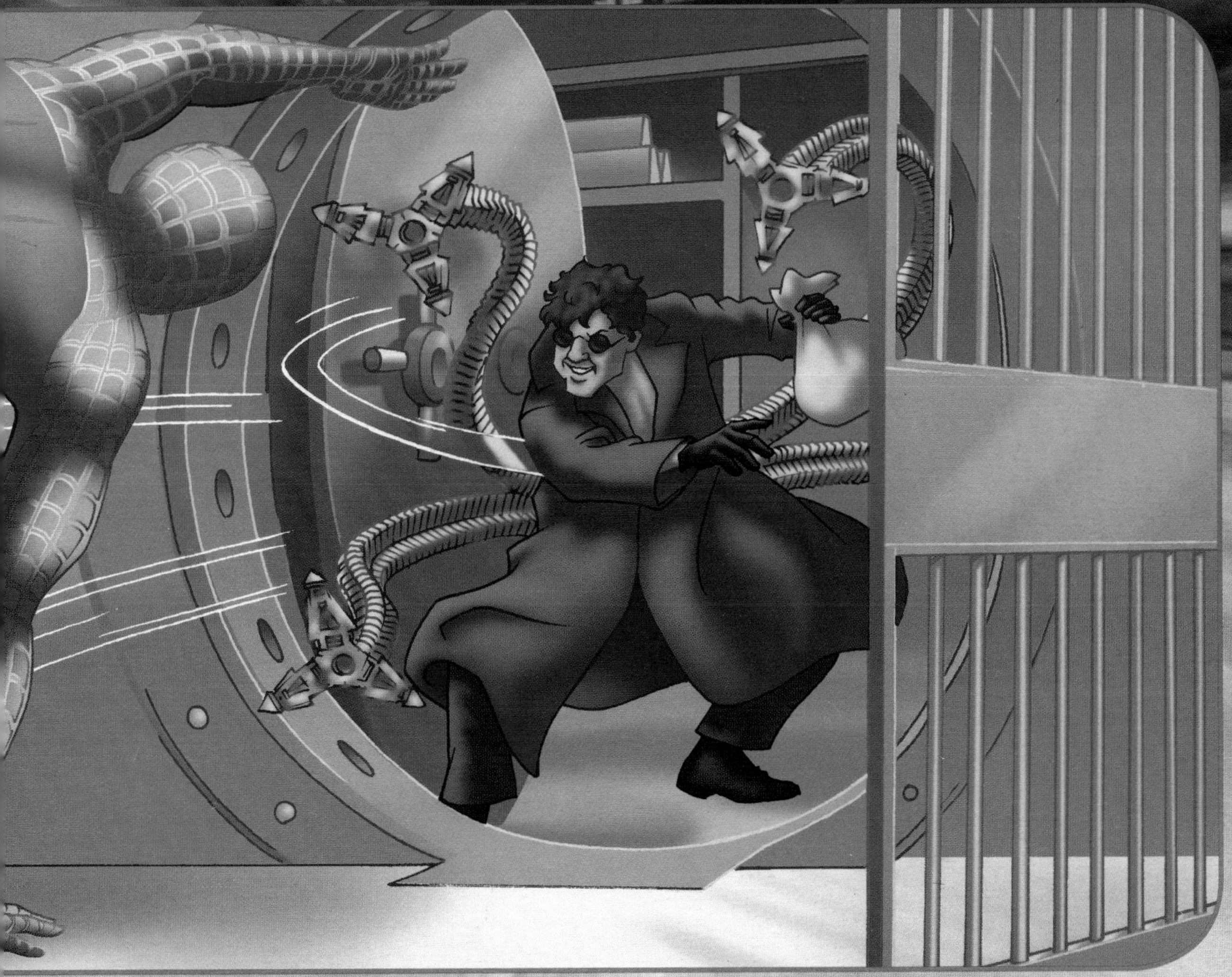

But Doc Ock was too fast for him. Soon Spider-Man crumpled to the floor.

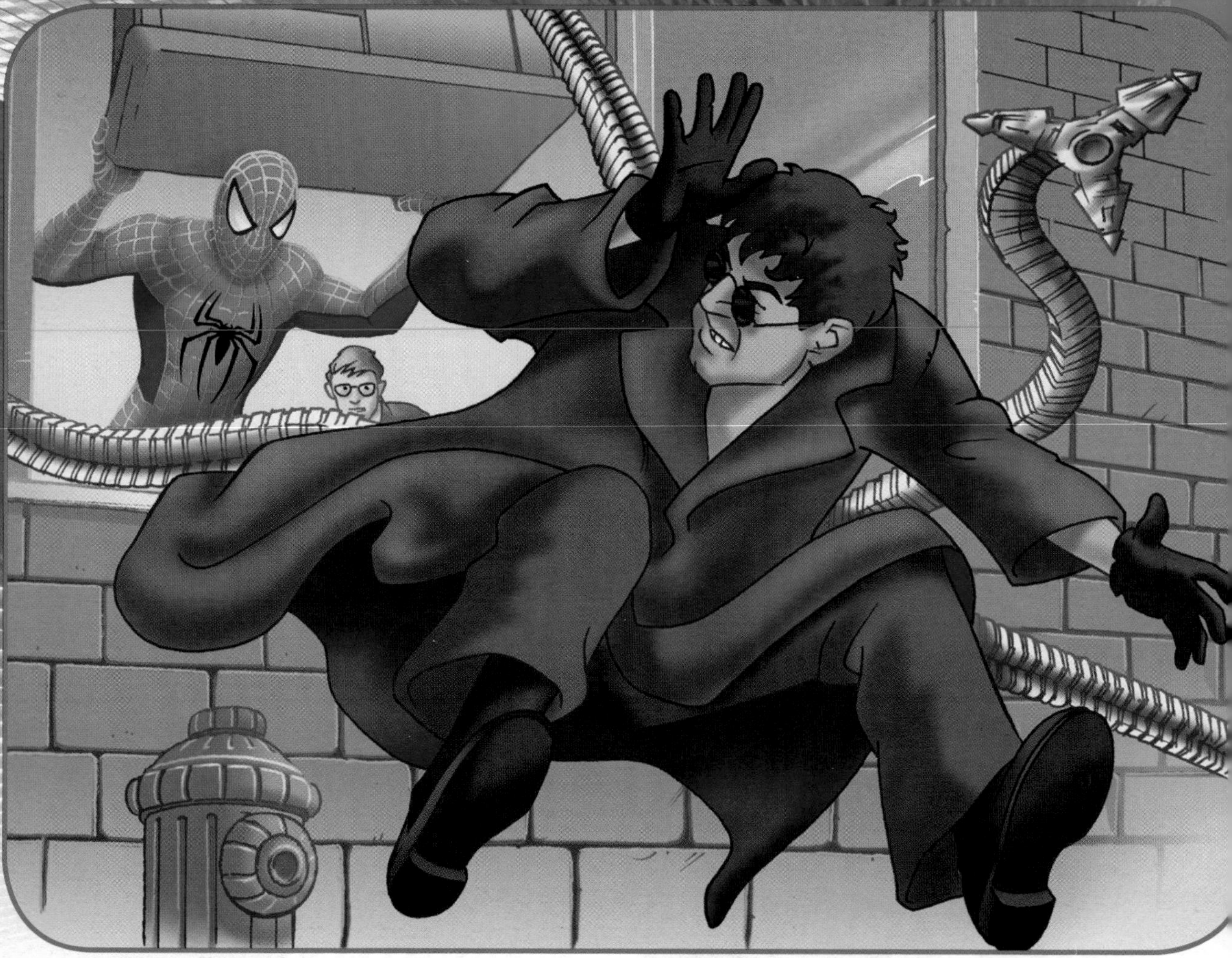

Doc Ock wrapped his tentacles around Spider-Man and squeezed! But he couldn't stop Spider-Man from firing webbing at a massive desk. Spider-Man flung the desk at Doc Ock and sent him flying through a window!

Doc Ock crash-landed onto the street. He roared in fury. He tossed a car in the air. Then he grabbed a girl and scrambled up the side of a building!

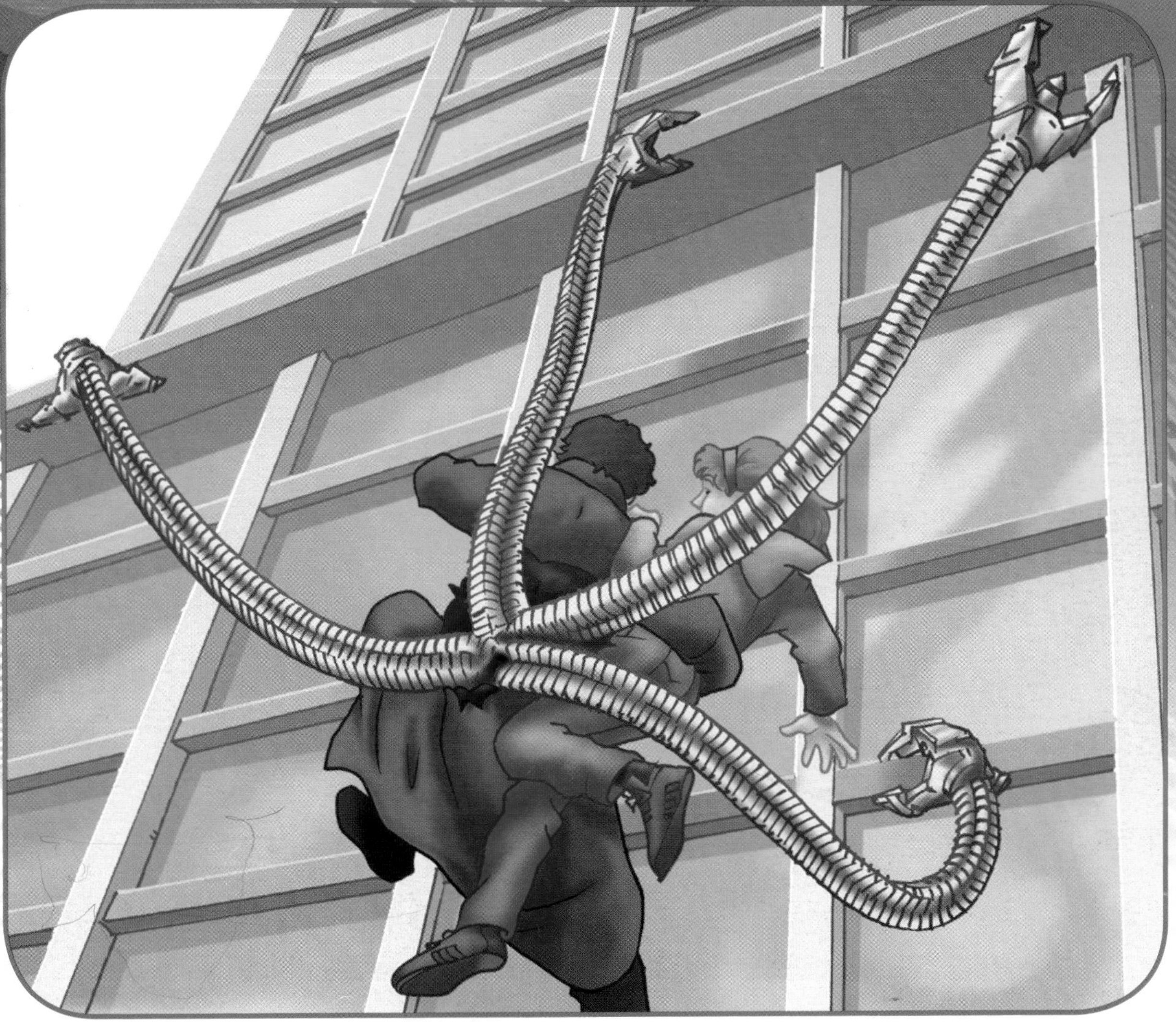

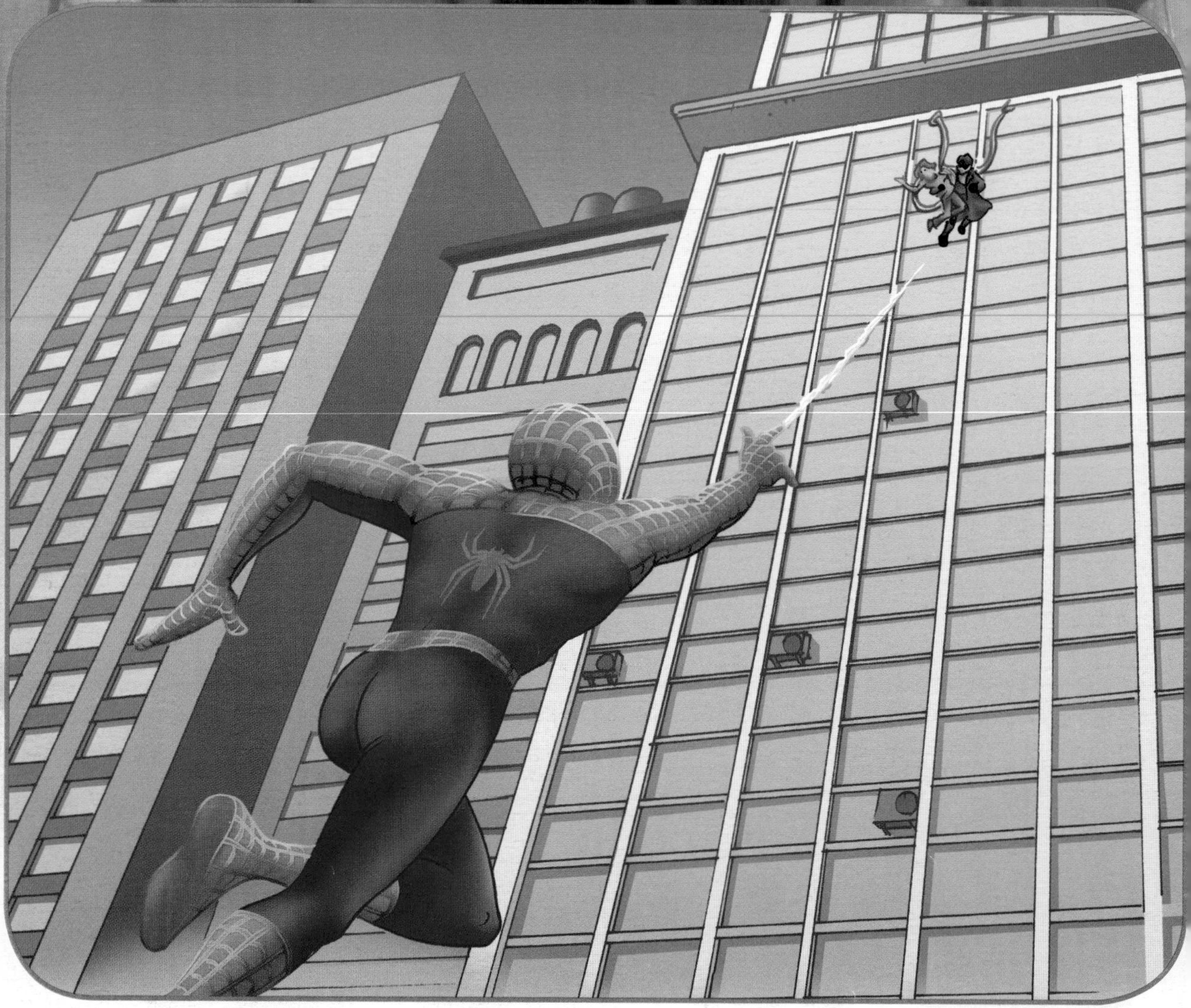

Spider-Man had stopped the robbery. Now he had to save the girl! Spider-Man fired a web and followed Doc Ock up.

"Set her down," he shouted.
Doc Ock bellowed, "Make me!"
So Spider-Man did.

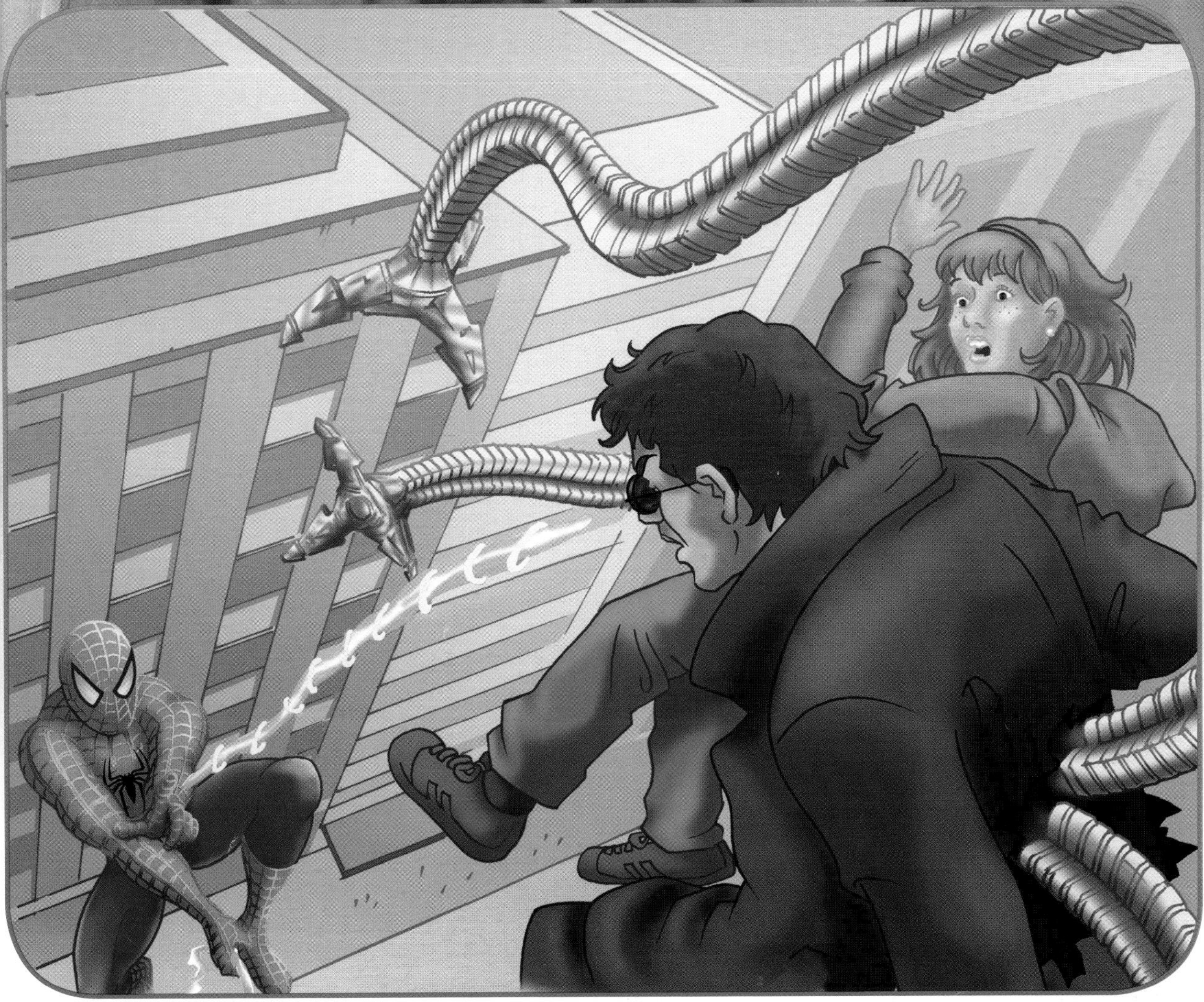

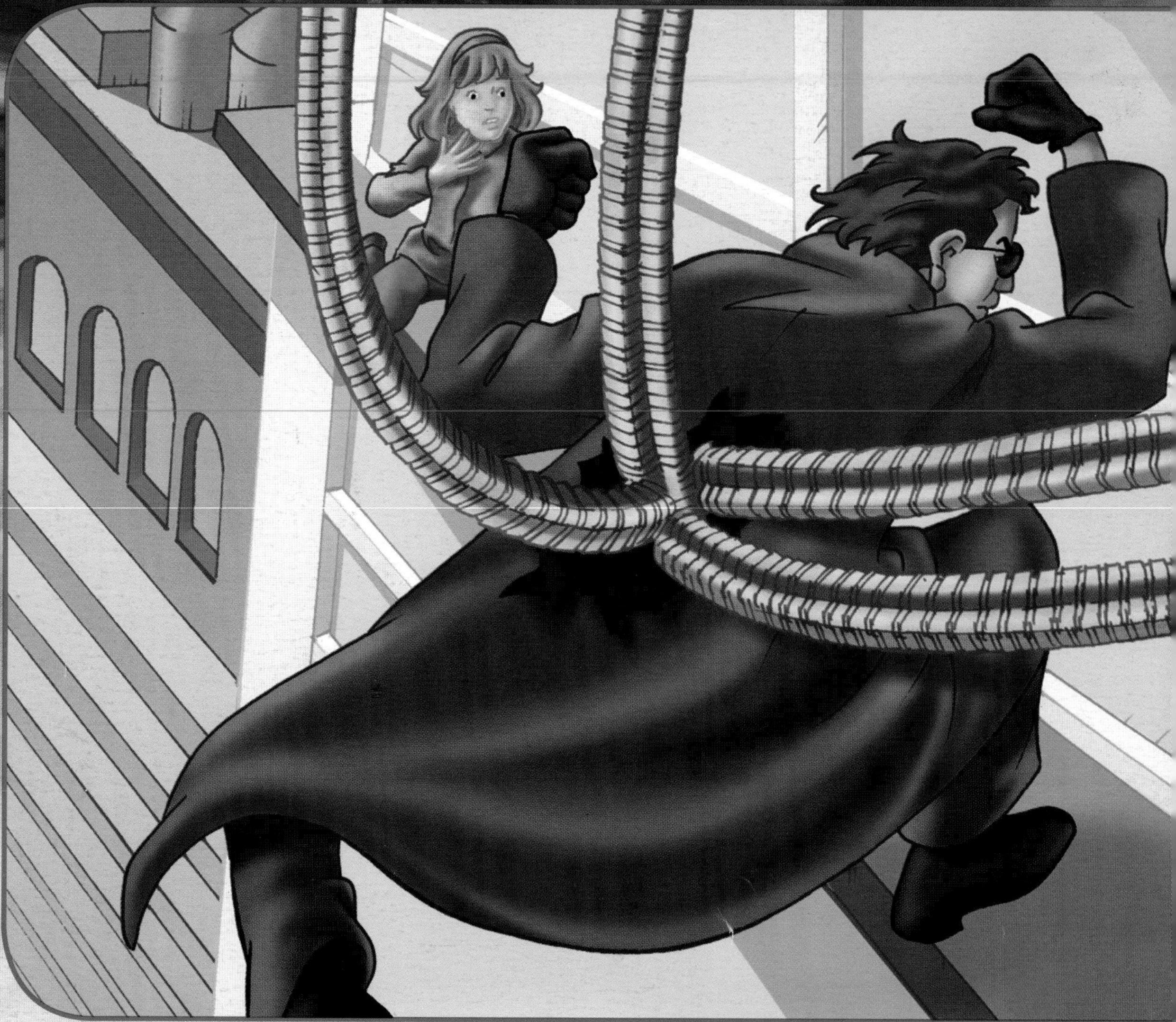

Spider-Man punched him, and Doc Ock lost his grip on the building. To get it back, he tossed the girl to a ledge. She barely managed to grab it. The girl was quivering with fear. She couldn't stay on for long. Spider-Man had to help her!

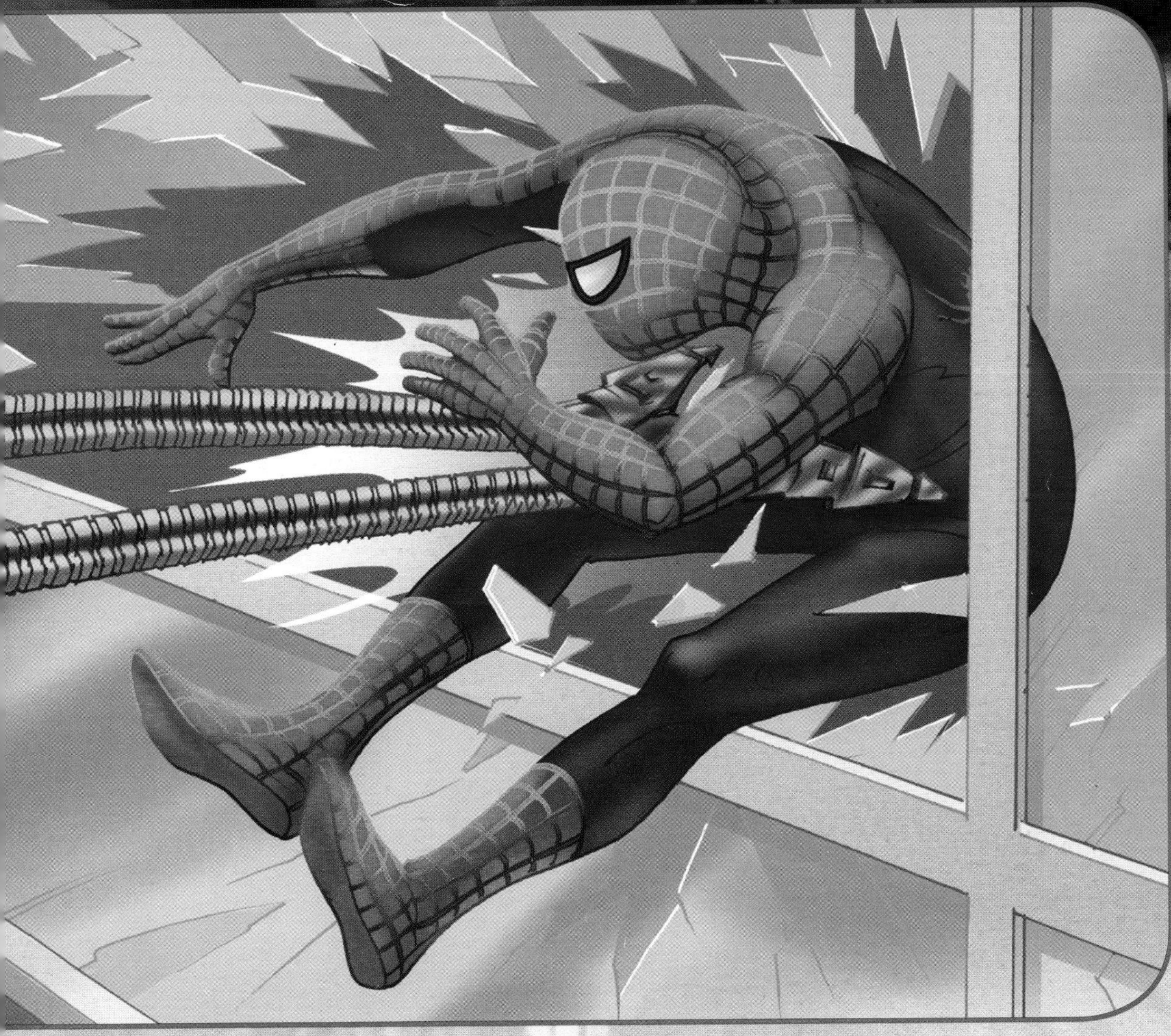

But he still hadn't shaken Doc Ock. The bad guy slammed Spider-Man with two of his lethal tentacles. His blow blasted Spider-Man through the side of the building!

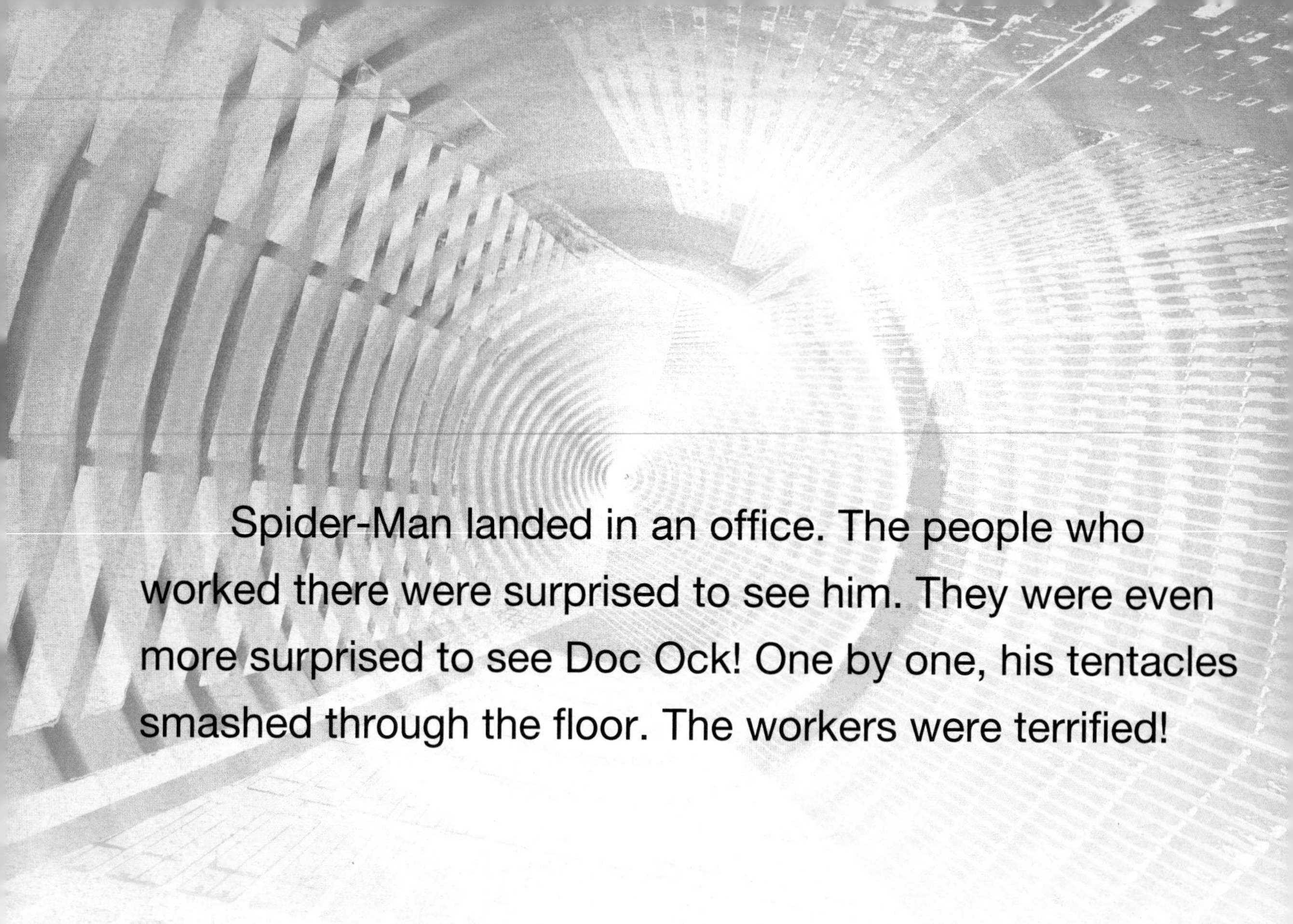

Spider-Man landed in an office. The people who worked there were surprised to see him. They were even more surprised to see Doc Ock! One by one, his tentacles smashed through the floor. The workers were terrified!

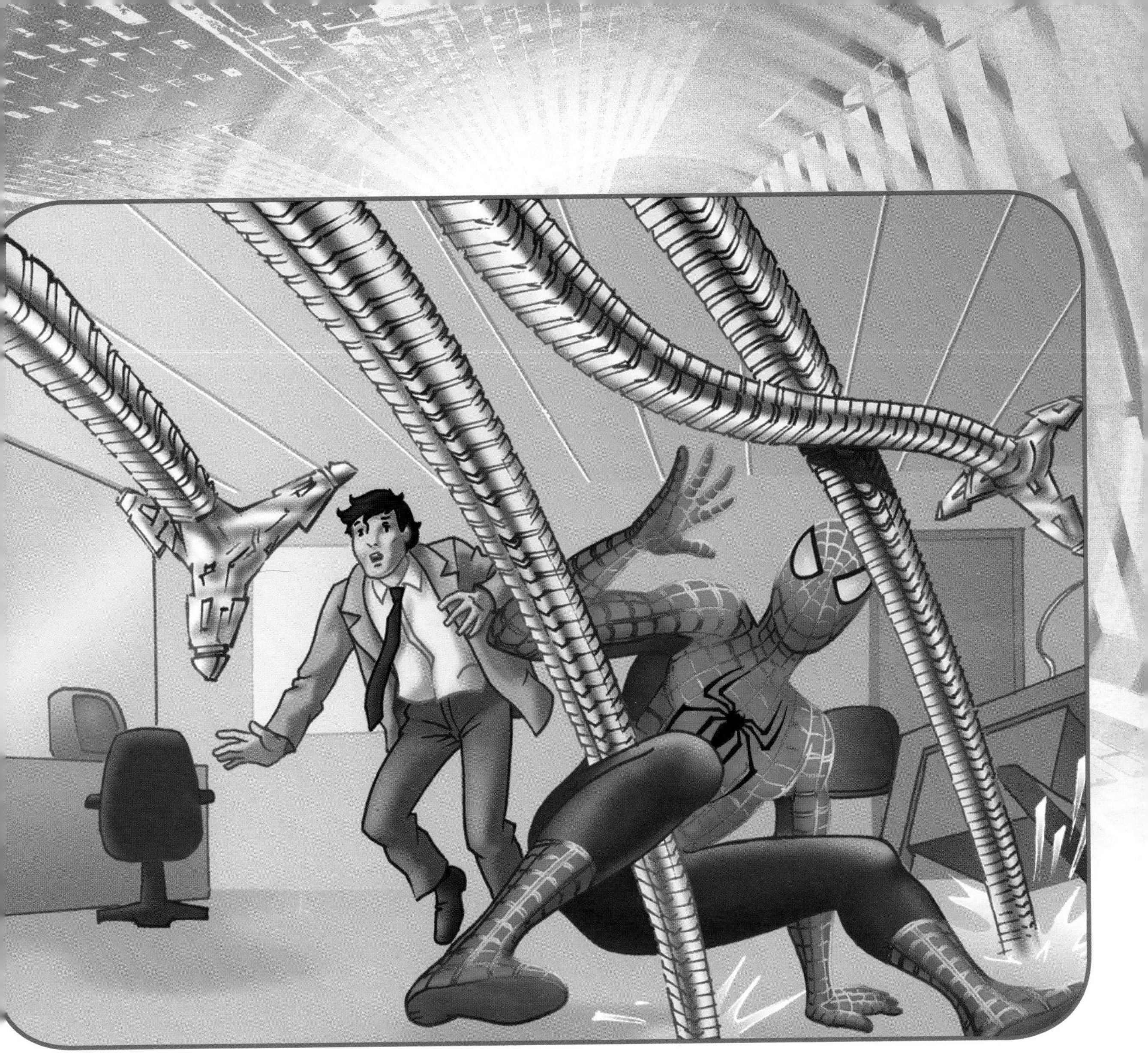

Spider-Man had Doc Ock by one tentacle when he heard a scream outside. He looked toward the ledge. Doc Ock had grabbed the girl with one of his other tentacles! He waved her in the air.

"Lose something?" he jeered.

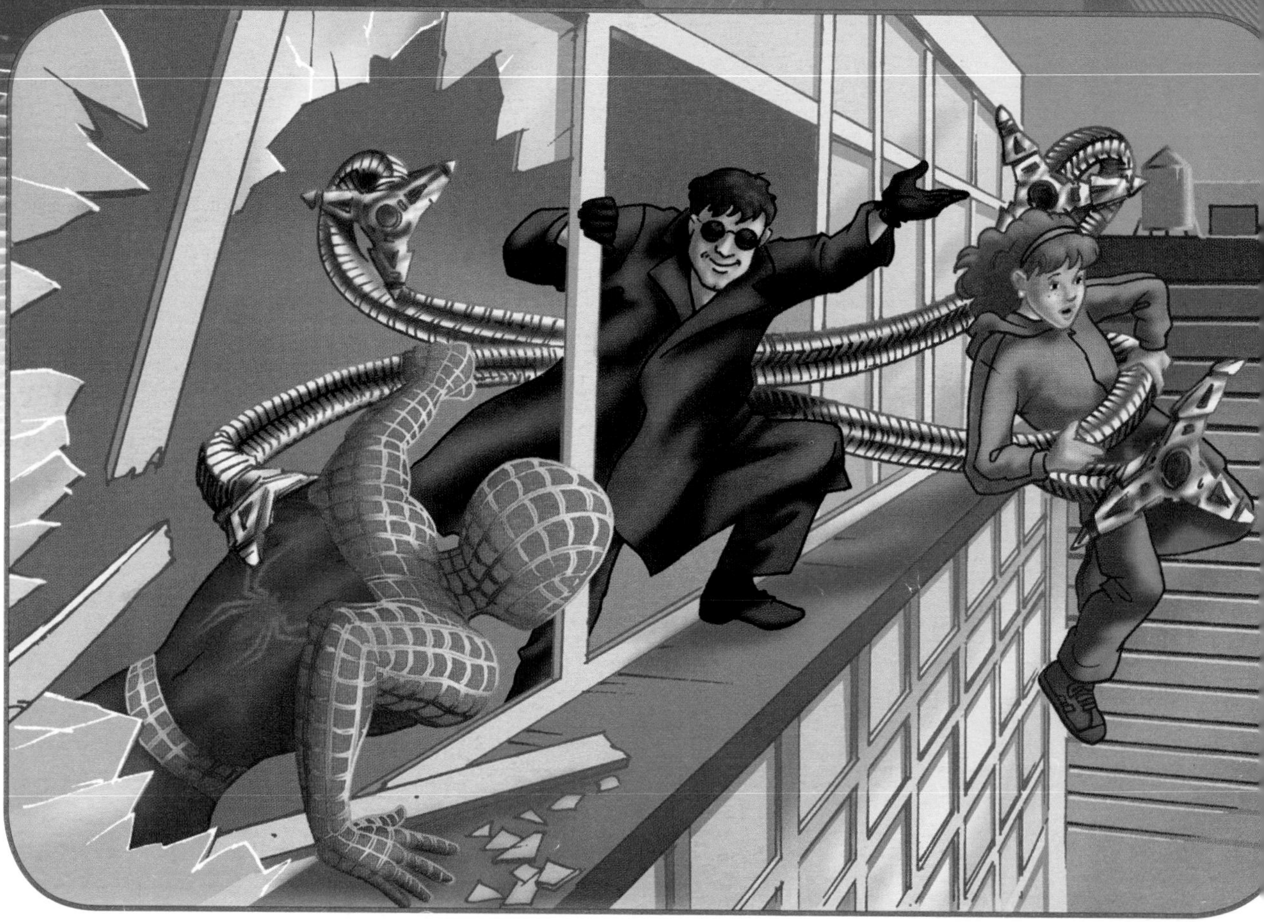

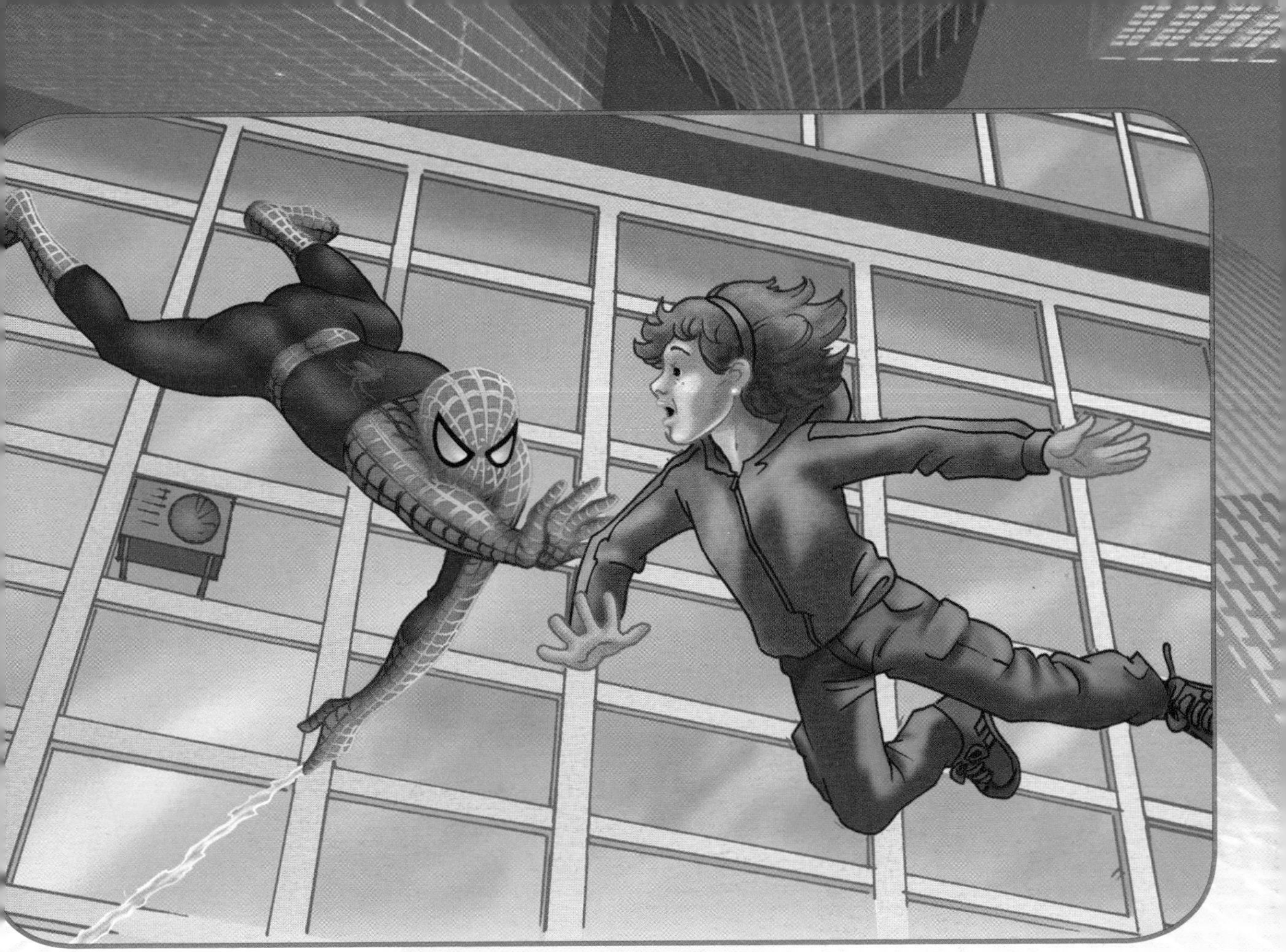

Spider-Man leaped toward the girl. He was prepared for a fight, and Doc Ock was ready for him. Suddenly the girl poked Doc Ock in the eye! Doc Ock screamed in pain and dropped her. Spider-Man caught her, and they soared away to safety.

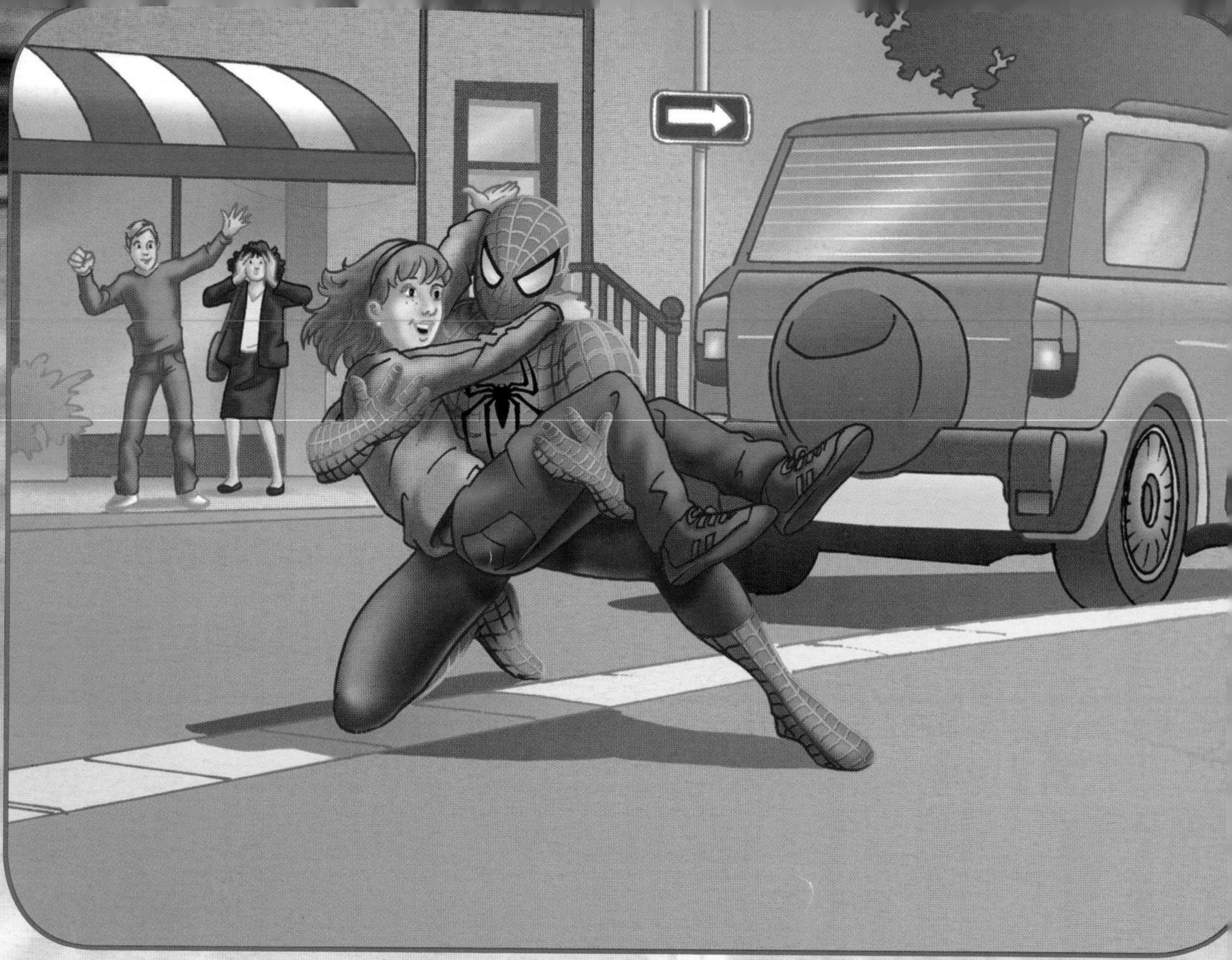

"We showed him!" said the girl when they landed.

Spider-Man stared at her. *We?* he thought. But he didn't say a word. Spider-Man didn't mind sharing the credit. Saving people was just part of his job. It was perfectly normal.